Presenting Tanya
the Ugly Duckling

Other books in the Tanya series:

Dance, Tanya

Bravo, Tanya

Tanya and Emily in a Dance for Two

Tanya Steps Out: A Book of Magical Moving Pictures

Tanya and the Magic Wardrobe

Text copyright © 1999 by Patricia Lee Gauch. Illustrations copyright © 1999 by Satomi Ichikawa

All rights reserved. This book, or parts thereof, may not be reproduced in any form without permission

in writing from the publisher, Philomel Books, a division of Penguin Putnam Books for Young Readers,

345 Hudson Street, New York, NY 10014. Philomel Books, Reg. U.S. Pat & Tm. Off.

Published simultaneously in Canada. Printed in Hong Kong by South China Printing Co. (1988) Ltd.

Book design by Gunta Alexander. The text is set in Horley Old Style.

Library of Congress Cataloging-in-Publication Data

Gauch, Patricia Lee. Presenting Tanya, the Ugly Duckling / Patricia Lee Gauch: illustrated by Satomi Ichikawa. p. cm.

Summary: When she has trouble mastering her dance steps in the part of the Ugly Duckling for the spring ballet recital,

Tanya is discouraged and fears that she has much in common with the character. [1. Ballet dancing—Fiction.

2. Self-perception—Fiction.] I. Ichikawa, Satomi, ill. II. Title. PZY.G2315Pr 1999 [E]—DC21 98-22266 CIP AC

ISBN 0-399-23200-1

1 3 5 7 9 10 8 6 4 2

First Impression

Presenting Tanya
the Ugly Duckling

BY PATRICIA LEE GAUCH

ILLUSTRATED BY SATOMI ICHIKAWA

PHILOMEL BOOKS ❖ NEW YORK

I am Tanya. Miss Foley says we will dance one whole ballet, *The Ugly Duckling*, in the spring recital. Mary Lou will dance the hunter, Mae Anne the cat, and Cynthia the wise swan. I will dance the ugly duckling, she says.

Why? I wonder. I am only Tanya.

That night in bed, I hear Miss Foley telling us the story: "It was a lovely, lovely summer day in the country when Mother Duck hatched her eggs, but the last was an ugly, ugly duckling.

"'What is that?' said an older duck. 'A turkey?'

"'No,' the mother duck said, 'my own dear duckling.'"

I know just how I will dance my part.

But at the next class Miss Foley gathers us around her
and teaches us steps. She tells us the other ducks pick on the
Ugly Duckling, the chickens peck at her, and the little girl
kicks her. We begin to dance.

"Be scared," she says to me, the Ugly Duckling.

But there are so many steps to learn, I forget to be scared:
*pas de chat, pas de chat, ballonné, brisé. Sissonne, sissonne,
soubresaut.*

I practice all the way home.

The ugly duckling wants to run away; I do, too.

"But there is a terrible thunderstorm," Miss Foley says as she plays the music at the next class. "Lightning flashes, the wind and rain blow. Ah, the poor little duckling. Where will she go?"

And I dance: *glissade, glissade, sissonne* to the front. I have learned every step.

But Miss Foley stops me. "Again, Tanya," she says.

I dance again: *glissade, glissade, sissonne* to the front.

"Again," Miss Foley says.

I try again! But Miss Foley pats my shoulder. "Patience, Tanya," she says.

What is wrong? I wonder. Poor duckling, poor me.

Many weeks go by. It is the end of autumn. Miss Foley starts the music one class. Violins play. Then she begins, "The leaves are turning yellow and falling. Crows are crying, caw, caw, caw. . . . The ugly duckling sees beautiful white birds flying away to the warm countries. But she is left behind in the middle of the pond."

The other dancers are dancing better and better. The *corps de ballet* of birds flitters and flies away, *sissonne, sissonne, sissonne.*

And I know all my steps, but I am still Tanya. I have two left feet and no wings at all. After class, I stay alone and practice.

Someone whispers, "Poor Tanya, she really is an ugly duckling."

There are only two weeks left before the spring recital. Miss Foley sits alone with me onstage next time we meet. "Tanya," she says, "snow is falling now. Can you see the snow? All the birds have left. See the empty sky? You are alone."

I am alone.

"But, wait, the water is freezing. The ice is closing around you. Turn, little duckling, turn."

I begin to turn, *fouetté, fouetté*.

"Faster, faster. The ice will catch you!"

I am suddenly cold. I turn and turn, but the ice is freezing around me. Until a farmer comes and saves me!

But Miss Foley cannot be onstage with me at the recital. And I am still Tanya until three days before the performance.

It is a dress rehearsal! We have on our costumes (I love my costume) and have danced through nearly the whole ballet. It is time for the last scene. The music plays. We can't even see Miss Foley, but then we hear her and dance out.

"The farmer's children tease and tease the ugly duckling. But one day, the duckling hears a lark. Spring has come, and out of the thicket floats a beautiful swan.

"The duckling knows that the swan may nip her or peck her. Afraid, she bows her head and floats toward the magnificent bird anyway, when she hears a voice say, 'Look into the pond.'"

I look into the pond.

"*Look*," the voice whispers again.

There is no duckling there. There is no Tanya there. There is only a beautiful young swan. It is me. I look around. All the trees are in bloom, the lilac and the apple, their branches touching the water. The wise old swan swims all around me. At first I only swim, stretching my wings.

Everyone watches: the hunter and the cat, the children and the farmer. Then other swans stroke me with their beaks, and a child says, "Oh, look, a new swan. The most beautiful of all."

And I spread my wings and rise into the air, circling the pond and circling it.

And now the pond is dark; the curtain comes down. I blink.
Miss Foley comes over to me and the other dancers and puts
her arms around our shoulders. "Yes," she whispers. "We are
ready for our performance now."

And I nod yes. I am ready, too.

Dance Term Glossary

Ballonné (from *ballon*): a ball-like or bouncing step that begins with
one leg in the air, and ends with it bent against the other leg.
Brisé (broken or breaking): a traveling jump in which the legs
execute a small beat.
Corps de ballet: the ensemble that dances in a group.
Fouetté (whipped): a turn on one leg, with the other leg whipping
the body around.
Glissade (to glide): a sliding step that begins and ends with a *plié*.
Pas de chat (step of the cat): a jump with both feet up, then both
feet down.
Plié (from *plier,* to bend): a bend with both knees out, heels in.
Sissonne (named for its originator): a scissor-like jump.
Soubresaut (a sudden spring or bound): a small jump straight up,
with both feet together.